The Cleverest Thief

as told by T.V. Padma

illustrated by Baird Hoffmire

Many years ago in a Buddhist monastery, there lived a great monk. For more than half of his one hundred years, he had guided the other monks, helping them lead lives of peace and service.

One day, the great monk fell ill. He had to choose someone to take his place as leader of the monastery.

He thought about each monk, but he could not decide.
He loved them all.

After a night of deep meditation, the leader called all the monks to gather around him.

He told them, "For many years we have lived and worked together as you have learned the teachings of the Buddha. Soon I will leave this world behind and one of you must take my place as leader."

"I could not choose among you, so I have a test to help me pick the next leader," the great monk said.

"Tonight I want each of you to steal something,"
he continued. "But you must steal it so gently that no one
will know who stole the item or how it was stolen."

"Think carefully over what I am saying and all I have taught you," the leader said. "The cleverest thief will take my place."

The monks were surprised, but each wanted to become the next leader, so they did not question him.

The monks began thinking about their task—all except one named Dhammika.

Dhammika asked softly, "How can you ask us to steal, wise one?"

The other monks cast disapproving looks at him. The leader was not angry. Instead, he said again, clearly, "I am asking you to steal so that no one can name the thief."

That evening, there was a strange feeling in the monastery. The monks kept a close watch on each other.

Some left for town, not to beg for an evening meal, but to steal. It was a restless night.

One of the monks slipped a necklace right off the neck of a wealthy woman.

Another stole a single grain of rice from a stall in the bazaar.

At dawn, even the birds seemed to twitter with excitement. The monks gathered around the leader carrying their stolen items—all except Dhammika.

The leader looked around and his eyes were sad. "Has each one of you stolen something?" he asked.
"No," said Dhammika. "I have brought you nothing."

Wanting to impress the leader, one monk spoke up. "I stole a grain of rice so it was not missed by anyone."

"I stole a necklace so quietly that the old lady did not feel it slipping off her neck. She will think it fell off on its own when she sees it is missing," said another.

The monks waved their stolen goods and shouted. The leader raised his hand for silence. "Dhammika, why are you empty-handed?" asked the leader.

"Sir, all night I thought of your instructions. I also thought of all that you have taught us over the years," answered Dhammika.

"You have told us to live without harming others, to defeat our greed, and to act with wisdom. Stealing did not seem right—not even if the prize was to be the new leader," said Dhammika.

"So I began to think deeply about your words," he continued. "You told us to steal so that no one could name the thief. This is impossible."

"Even if I lied to everyone, I could never keep my actions a secret from myself. I would be the thief and I would always know it," Dhammika finished.

The monks nodded, seeing the truth in Dhammika's words. The leader smiled and said, "Yes, you may hide your actions from the world, but never from yourself."

The leader turned to Dhammika and said, "You, alone, stayed true to yourself and to my teachings. You will be the next leader."

The great monk sighed deeply, pleased with his choice.

All the other monks bowed to Dhammika, their new guide.

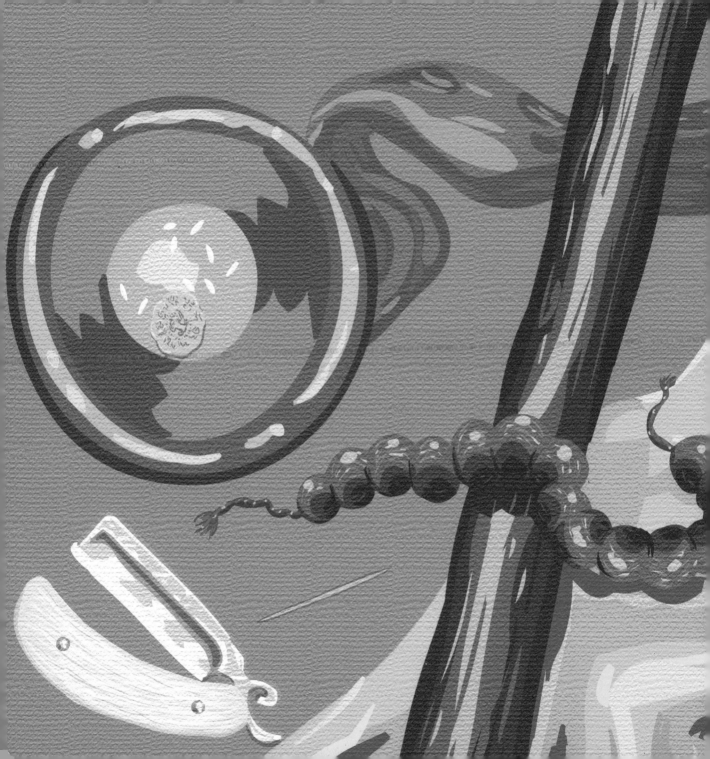